A Home

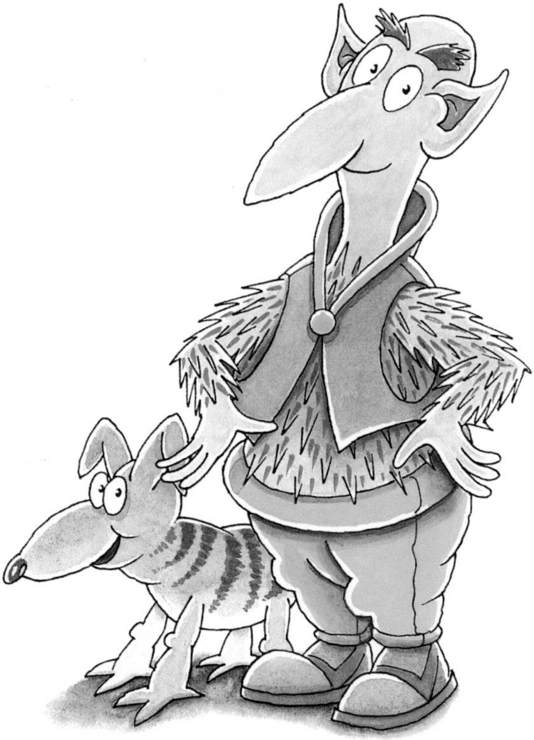

Illustrated by Clive Taylor

Rigby

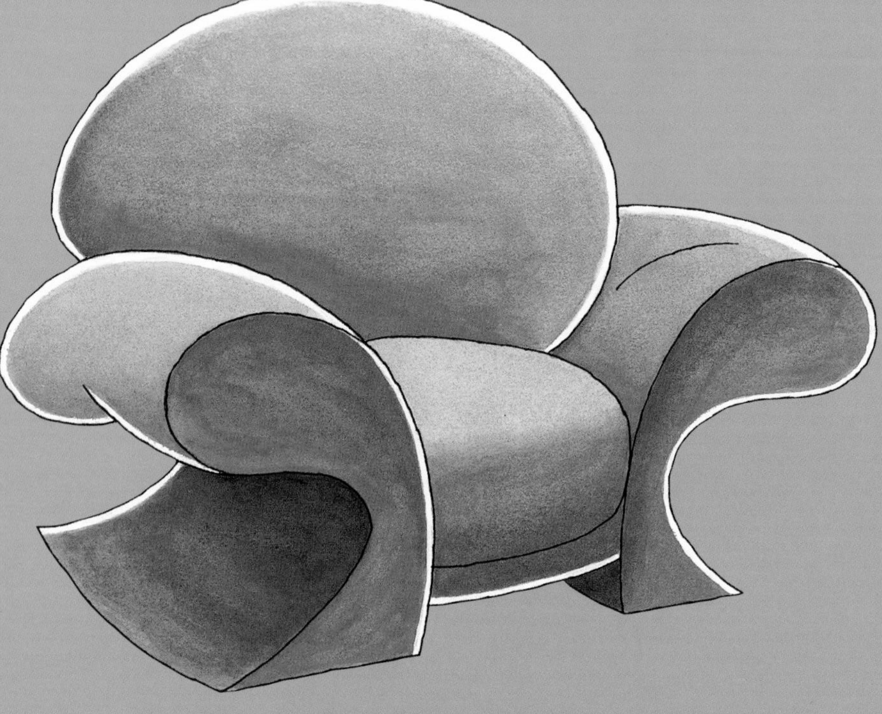

a chair

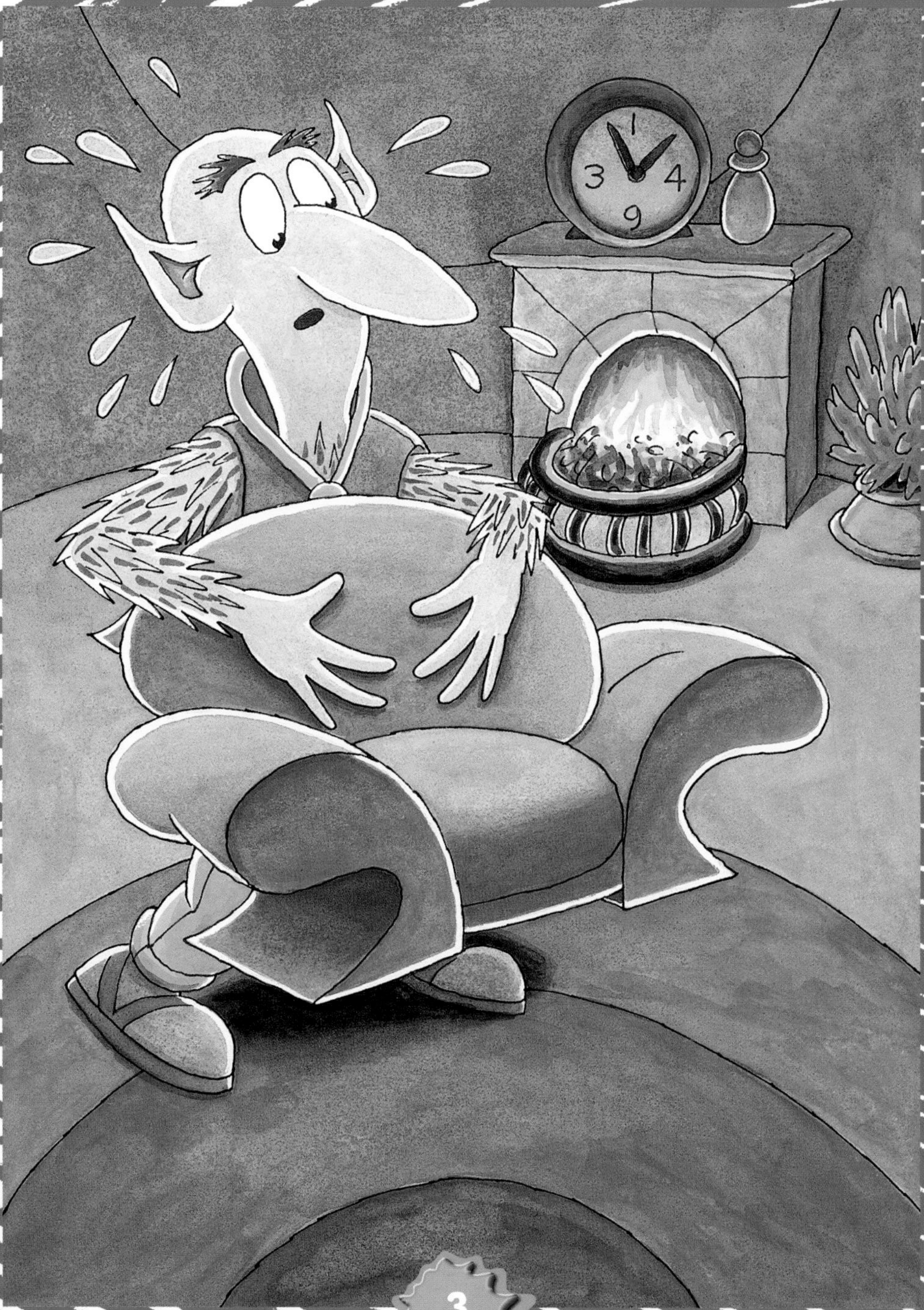
1
3
4
9

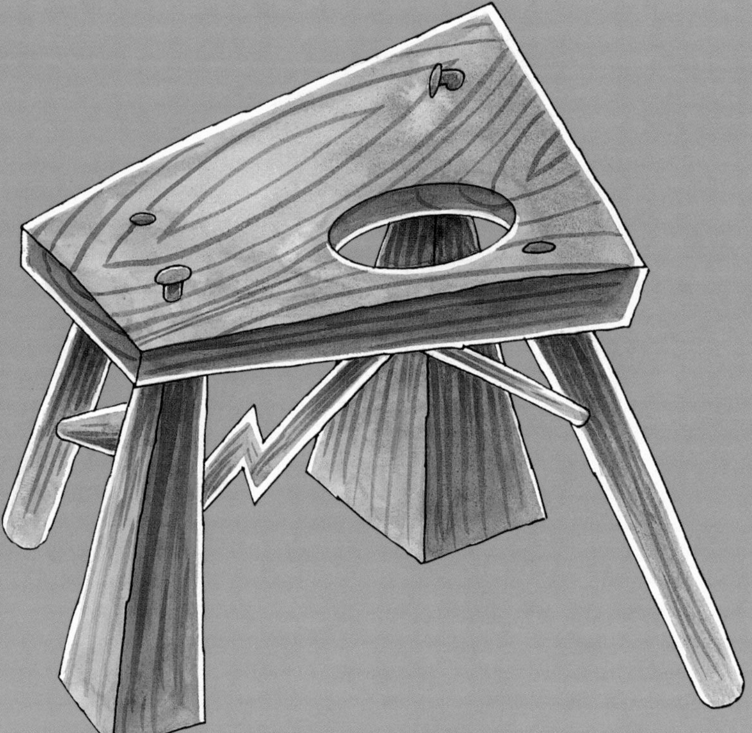

a table

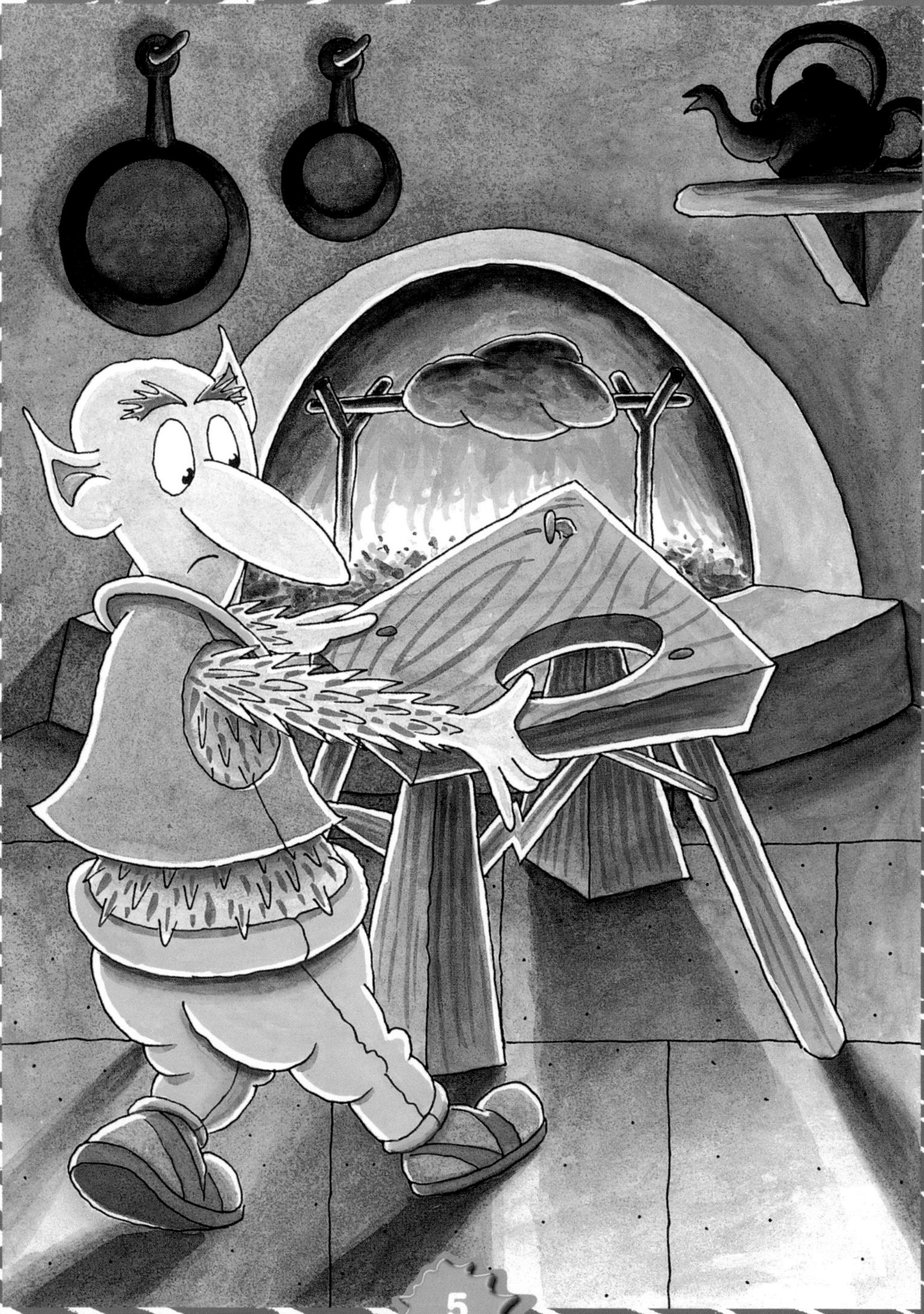

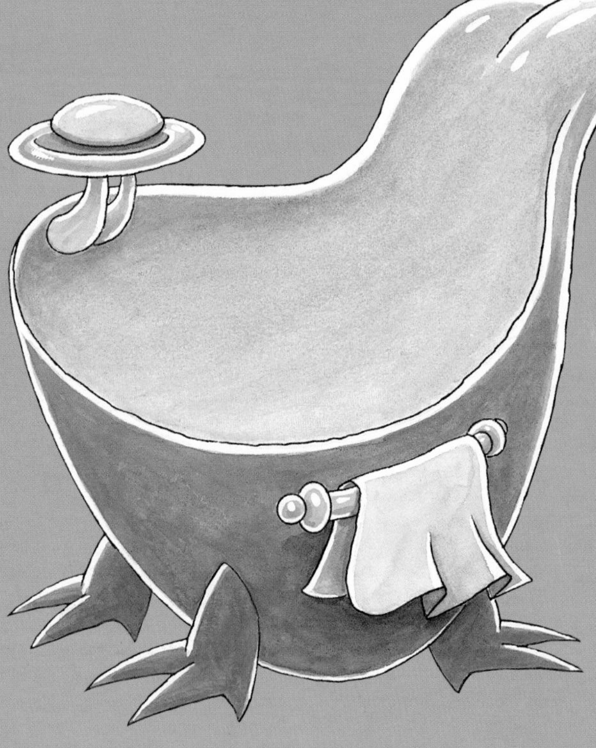

a bathtub

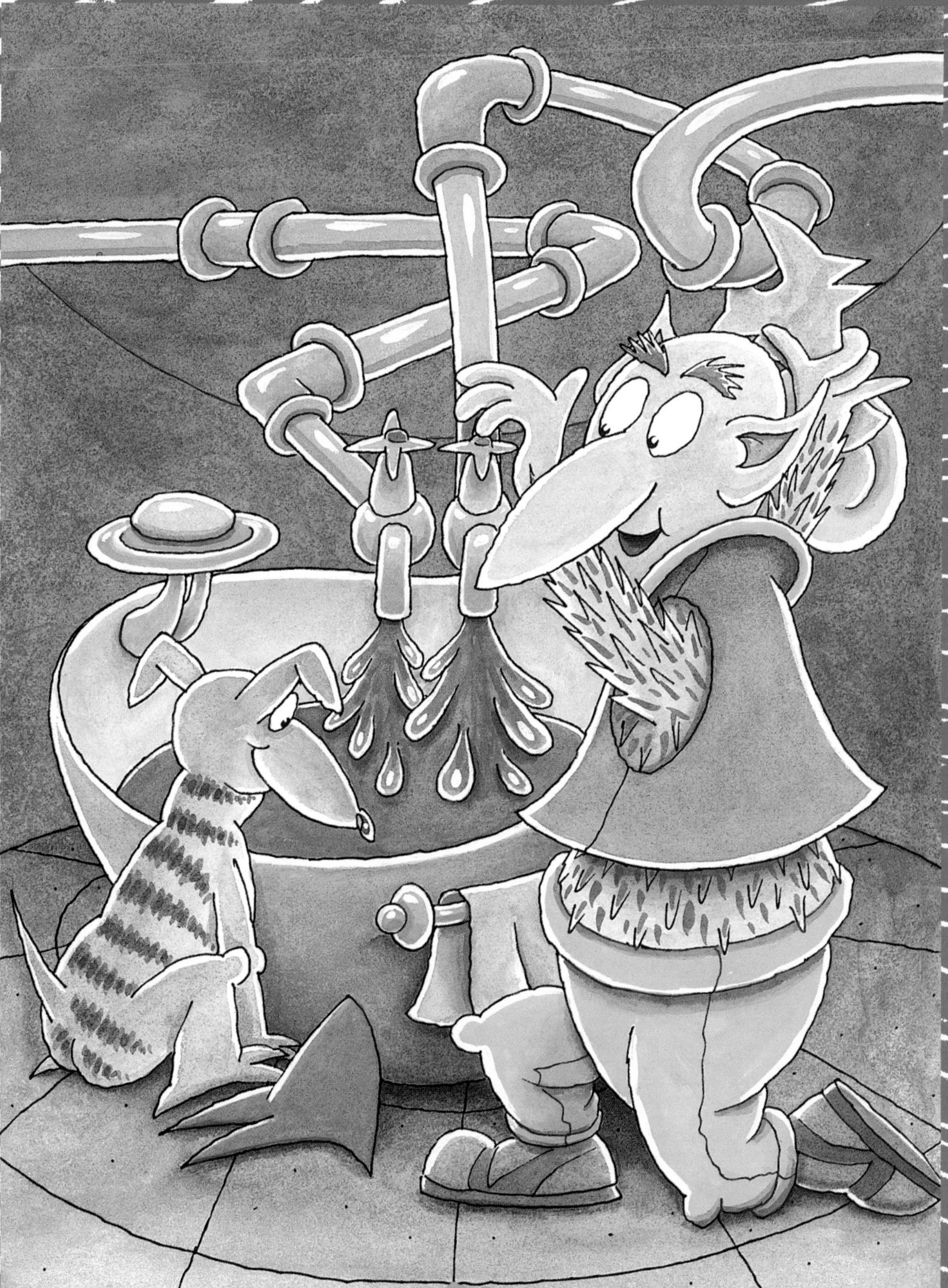

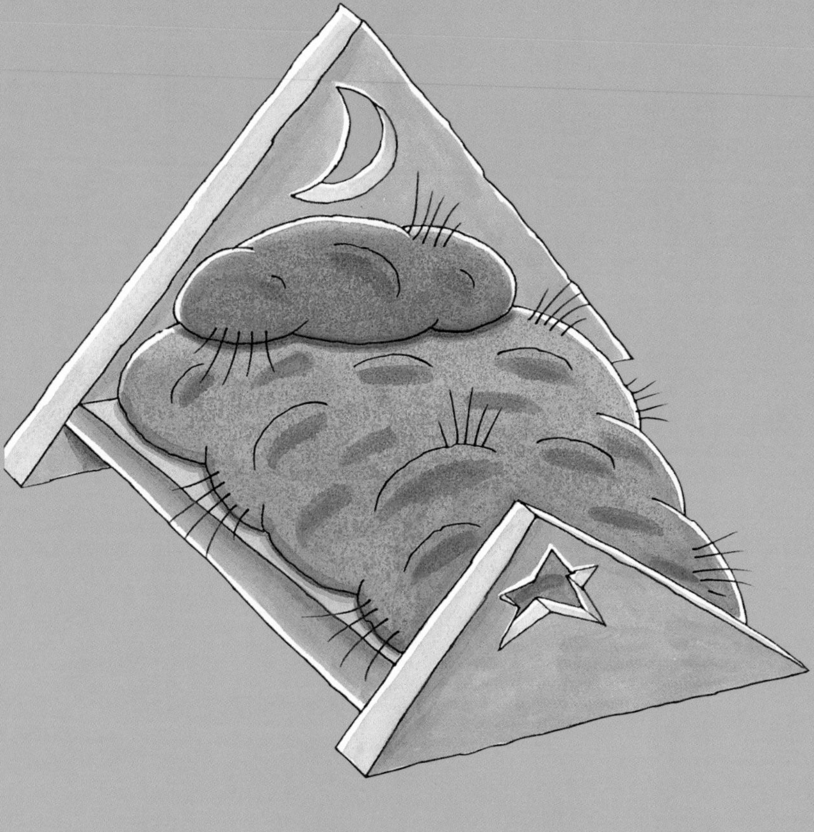

a bed

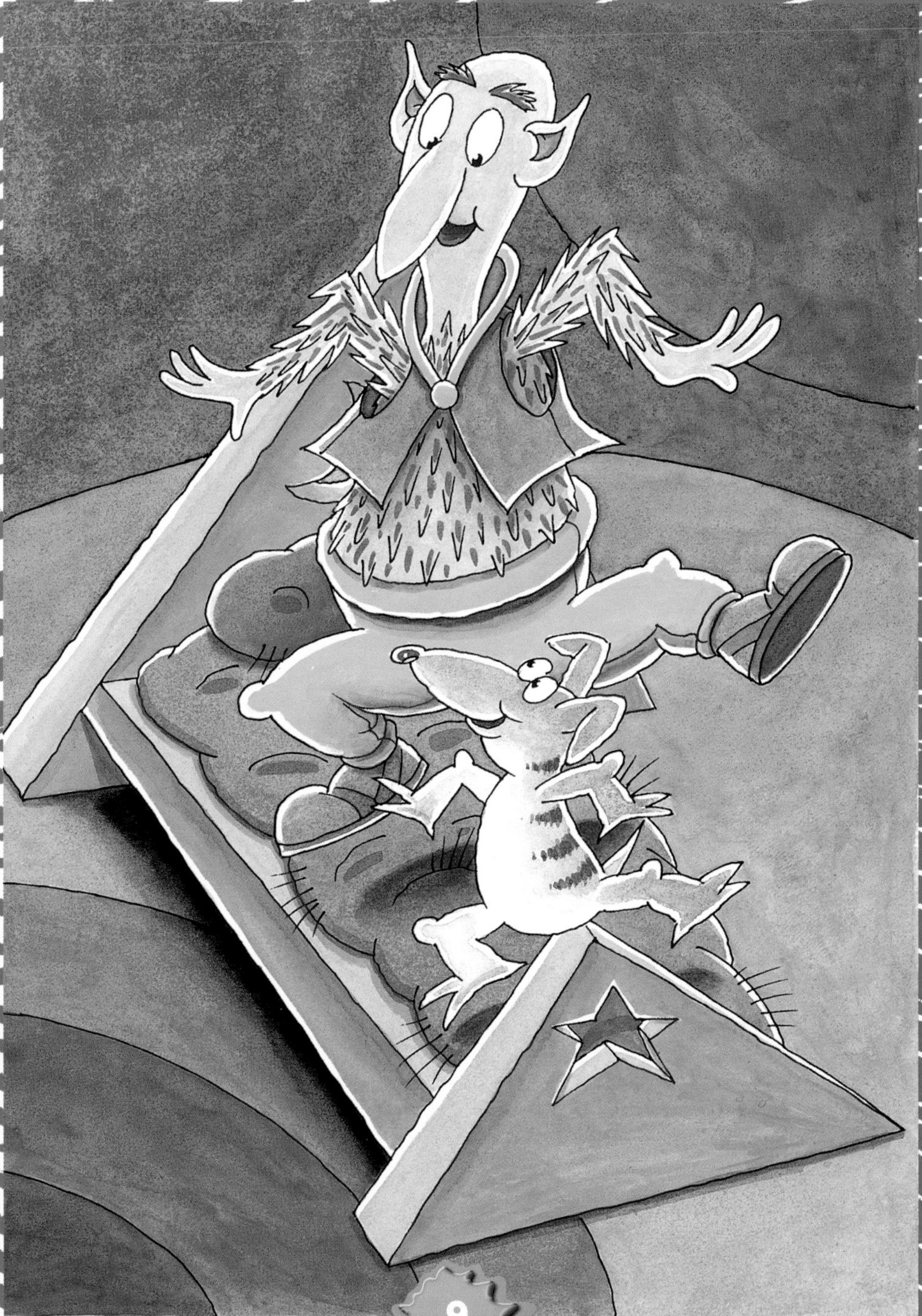

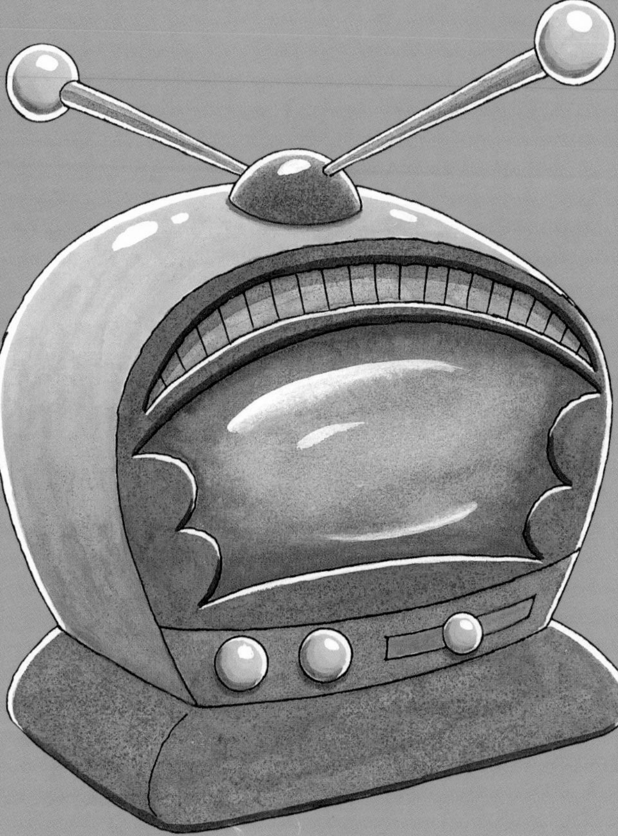

a television

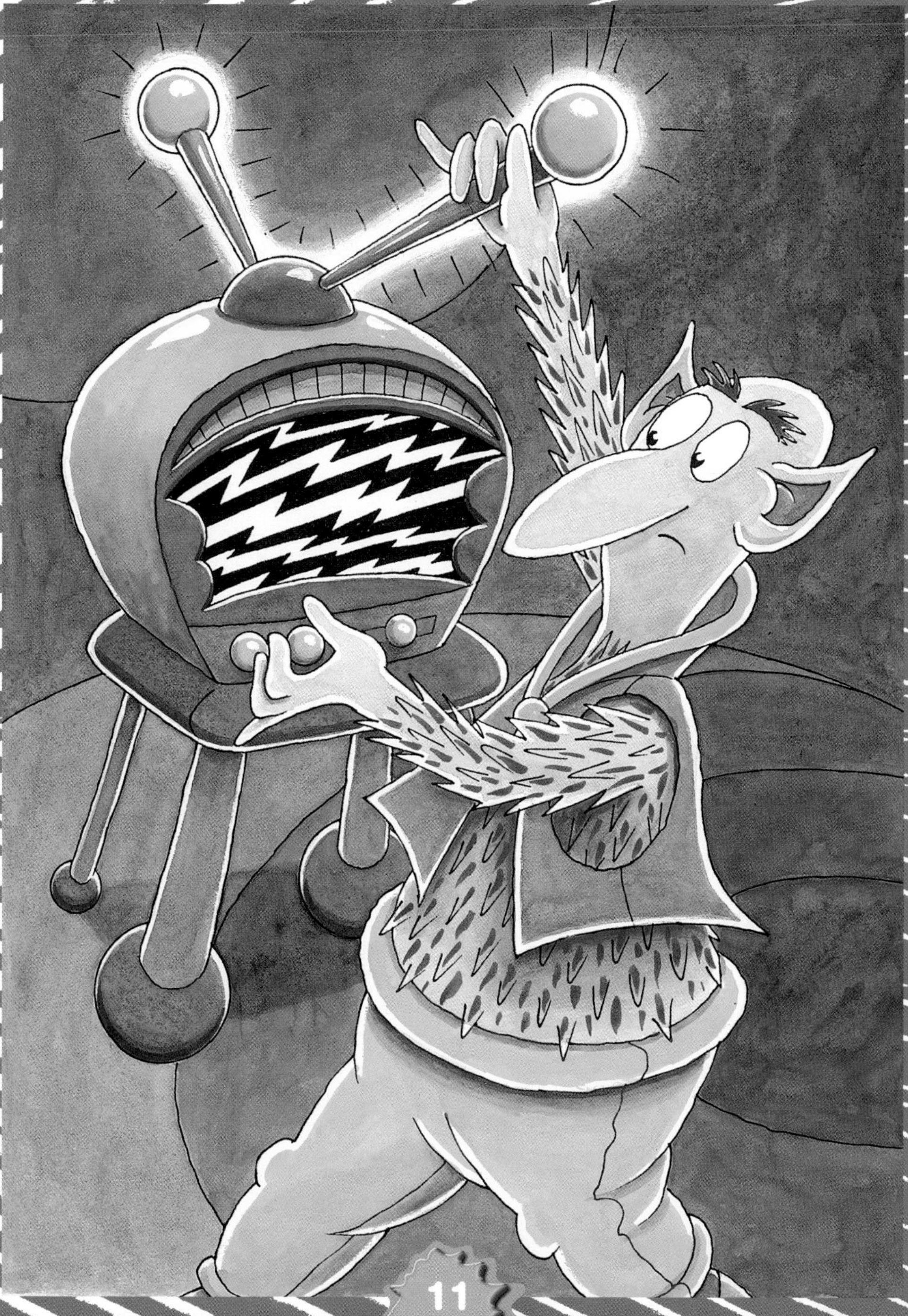

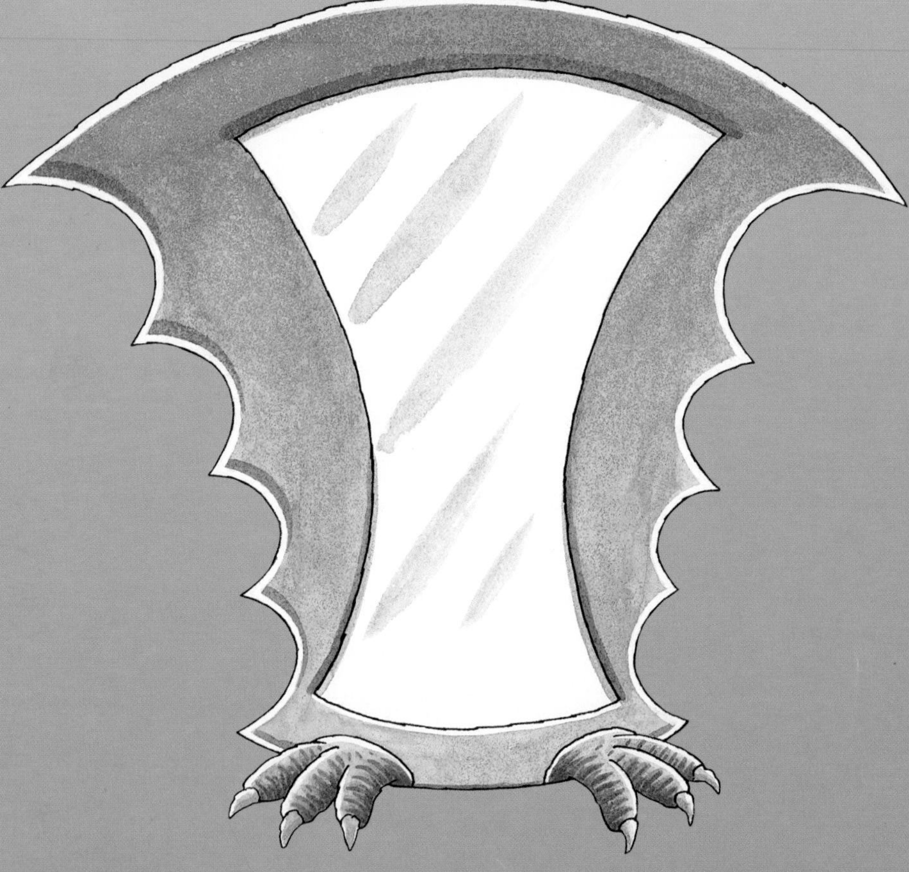

a mirror

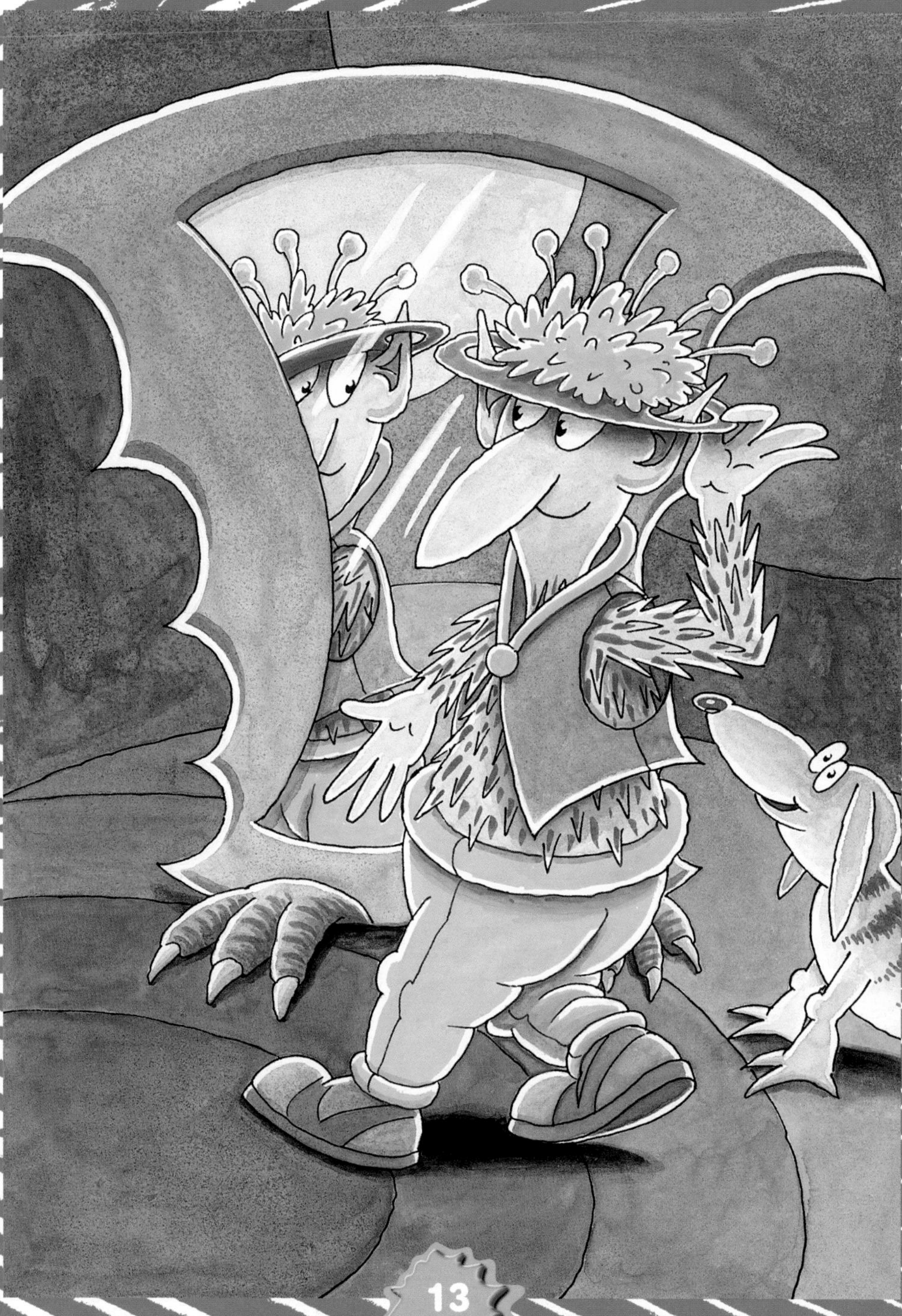

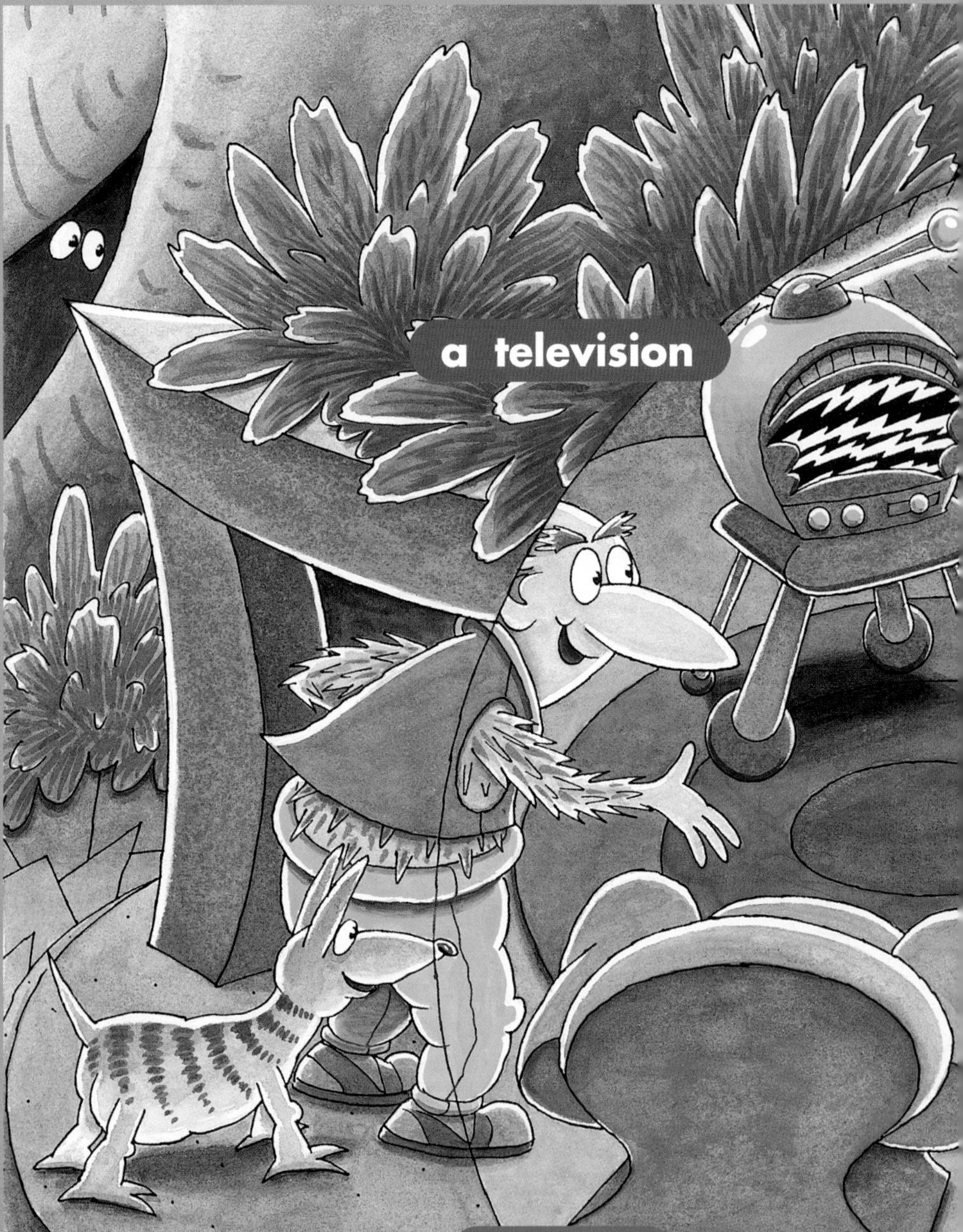
a television
a chair

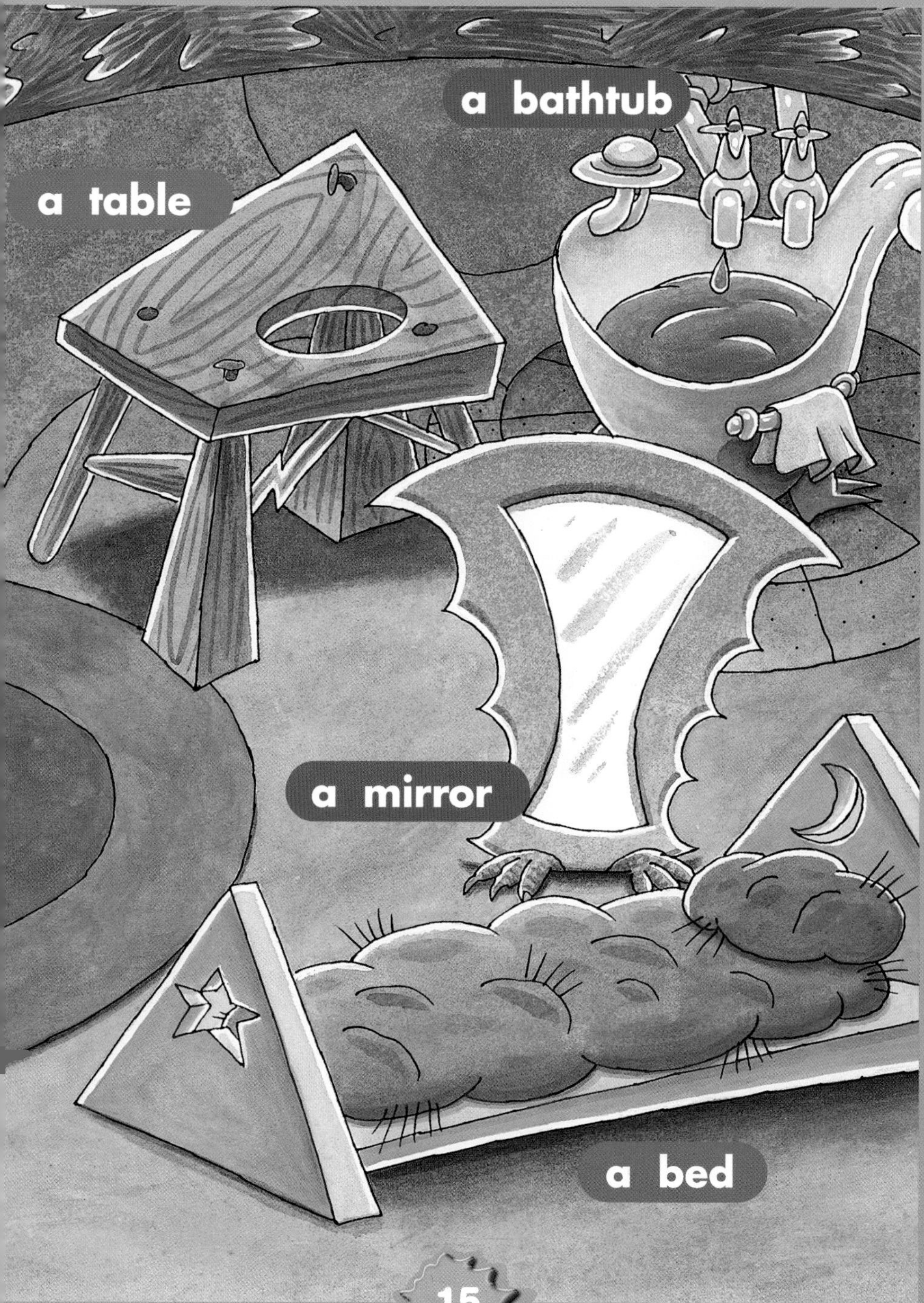
a bathtub
a table
a mirror
a bed

a

the

my

a

is